Winnie-the-Pooh and Friends

Piglet Does A Very Grand Thing

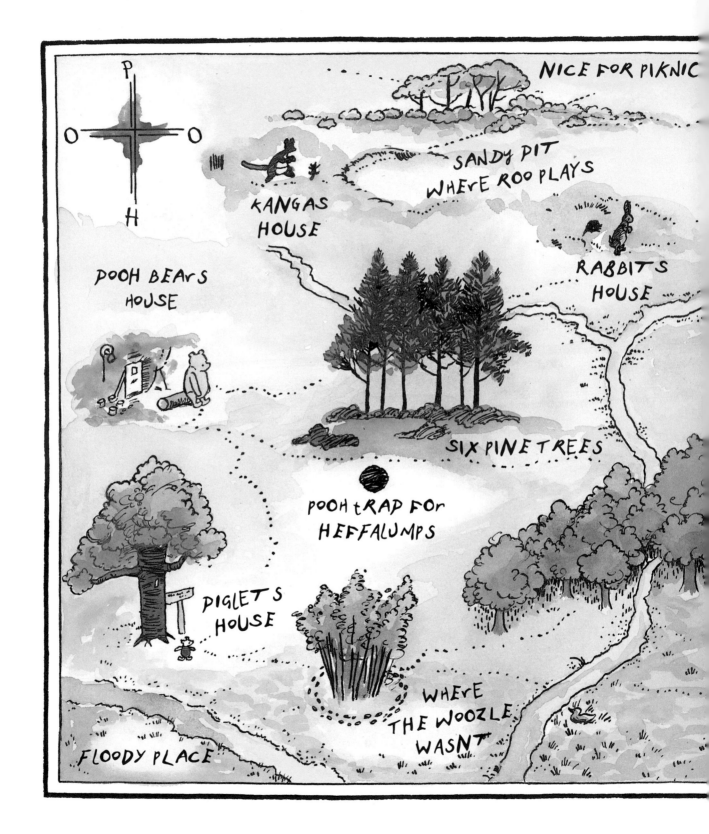

"I wish to pay tribute to the work of E.H. Shepard
which has been inspirational in the creation
of these new drawings."
Andrew Grey

DEAN

This edition first published in Great Britain in 2014
by Dean, an imprint of Egmont UK Limited
The Yellow Building, 1 Nicholas Road, London W11 4AN
© 2019 Disney Enterprises, Inc
Based on the Winnie-the-Pooh works by A. A. Milne and E. H. Shepard
Illustrations by Andrew Grey

ISBN 978 0 6035 7010 0
58230/003
Printed in Great Britain

Piglet Does A Very Grand Thing

One windy autumn morning, Pooh and Piglet were sitting in their Thoughtful Spot.

"What *I* think," said Pooh, "is we'll go to Pooh Corner and see Eeyore. In fact, let's go and see everybody."

Piglet thought they ought to have a Reason
for seeing everybody if Pooh could think of
something. Pooh could.
"We'll go because it's Thursday," he said. "We'll wish
everybody a Very Happy Thursday."

By the time they got to Kanga's house they were so buffeted by the wind that they stayed to lunch.

It seemed rather cold
outside afterwards,
so they pushed on
quickly to **Rabbit's**.
"We've come to wish
you a **Very Happy
Thursday**," said Pooh.

"Oh I thought you'd
really come about
something,"
Rabbit said.
They sat down for
a little . . . and
by-and-by Pooh
and Piglet went
on again.

Christopher Robin was so glad to see them that they stayed until very nearly tea time, and had a **Very Nearly** tea. Then they hurried on to Pooh Corner, to see **Eeyore** before it was too late to have a **Proper Tea** with Owl.

"Hallo, Eeyore. We came to see how your house was,"
said Piglet. "Look, Pooh, it's still standing!"
"I know," said Eeyore.
"Well, we're **very glad** to see you, Eeyore, and now
we're going on to see Owl," said Pooh.
"Goodbye," said Eeyore. "Mind you don't get **blown
away,** little Piglet."

The **wind**
was against
them now,
and Piglet's ears **streamed**
out behind him like banners.
It seemed like hours
before he got them
into the shelter
of the Hundred
Acre Wood.

In a little while they were knocking and ringing
cheerfully at **Owl's door.**

"Hallo, Owl," said Pooh. "I hope we're not too late
for – I mean, how are you, Owl?"

"Sit down," said Owl kindly. "Make yourselves comfortable."

They made themselves as comfortable as they could. "Am I right in supposing that it is a **very Blusterous day** outside?" Owl said.

"Very," said Piglet, who was quietly **thawing** his ears.

"I thought so," said Owl. "It was on just such a **Blusterous day** that my Uncle Robert, a portrait of whom you see upon the wall – What's that?"

There was a **loud cracking noise.**

"Look out!" cried Pooh. "Piglet, I'm falling on you!" The room was slowly **tilting upwards.** The clock slithered along the mantelpiece, collecting vases on the way, until they all **crashed** together on to what had once been the floor, but was now trying to see what it looked like as a wall.

For a little while it became **difficult** to remember which was really the north. Then there was another **loud crack** . . . and there was **silence**.

In the corner of the room,
the table-cloth wrapped
itself into a ball
and **rolled** across
the room.

It **jumped** up
and down and
put out two ears.

Then it **unwound**
itself, revealing
Piglet.

"Pooh," said Piglet nervously. "Are we still in Owl's house?"

"I think so."

"Oh!" said Piglet. "Well, did Owl *always* have a letter-box in his ceiling? Look!"

"I can't," said Pooh. "I'm face downwards under something, and that, Piglet, is a very bad position for looking at ceilings."

Owl and Piglet pulled at the chair and in a little
while Pooh came out.
"What are we going to do, Pooh?" asked Piglet.
"Well, I *had* just thought of something," said Pooh.
And he began to sing:

I lay on my chest
And I thought it best
To pretend I was having an evening rest;

I lay on my tum
And I tried to hum
But nothing particular seemed to come.

My face was flat
On the floor, and that
Is all very well for an acrobat;

But it doesn't seem fair
To a Friendly Bear
To stiffen him out with a basket-chair.

And a sort of sqoze
Which grows and grows
Is not too nice for his poor old nose,
And a sort of squch
Is much too much
For his neck and his mouth
and his ears and such.

Owl coughed and said that if Pooh was sure
that was all, they could now give their minds to the
Problem of Escape.

"Could you fly up to the letter-box with Piglet on your
back?" Pooh asked.
"No," said Piglet quickly. "He couldn't."
Pooh's mind went back to the day when he had saved
Piglet from the flood, and everybody had admired
him so much. Suddenly, just as it had come before,
an idea came to him.

"I have thought of something," said Pooh. "We tie a piece of string to Piglet. Owl flies up to the letter-box, with the other end in his beak, pushes it through the wire and brings it down to the floor. We pull hard at this end, and Piglet goes slowly up at the other end."

"And there he is," said Owl. "If the string doesn't break."

"Supposing it does?" asked Piglet.

"It won't break," whispered Pooh comfortingly, "because you're a Small Animal, and I'll stand underneath, and if you save us all, it will be a Very Grand Thing to talk about afterwards."

Piglet felt **much better**, and when he found himself going up to the ceiling, he was **so proud** that he would have called out 'Look at me!' if he hadn't been **afraid** that Pooh and Owl would let go of their end of the string to look at him.

Soon it was over.

Piglet opened
the letter-box and
climbed out.

He turned to squeak
a **last message** to
the prisoners.

"It's all right," he called. "Your tree is blown right over, Owl, and there's a branch across the door. I will be back in about half an hour with Christopher Robin. Goodbye, Pooh!" And without waiting to hear Pooh's answering, "Goodbye and thank you," he was off.

"Half an hour," said Owl. "That will just give me time to finish that story I was telling you about my Uncle Robert – a portrait of whom you see underneath you. Now let me see, where was I? Oh, yes. It was on just such a Blusterous day as this that my Uncle Robert–"
Pooh closed his eyes.

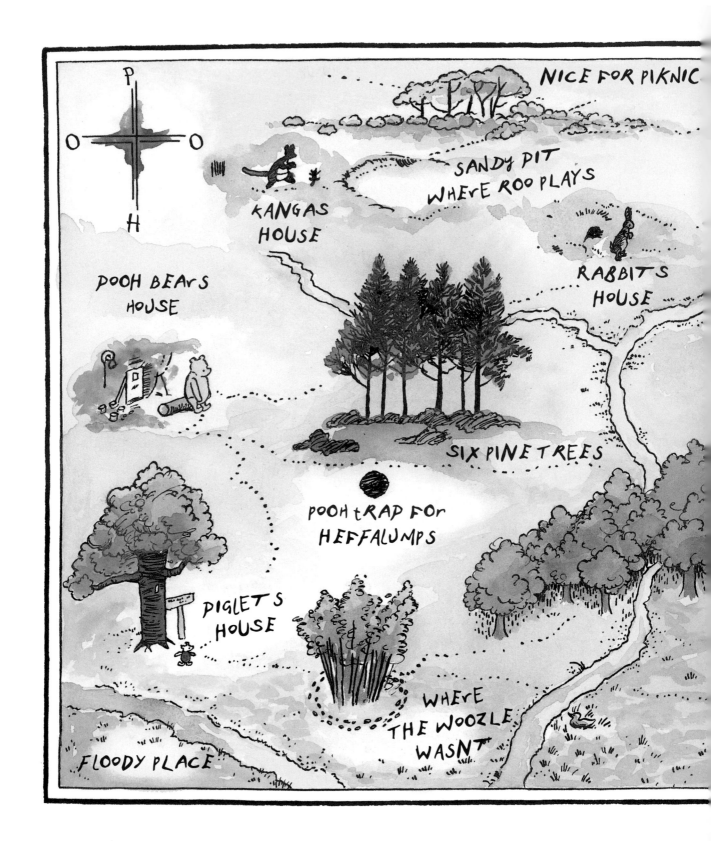

Good bye.